Brave
Danny

Written by

Robin Adolphs

Illustrated by

Nicky Johnston

Published by Butternut Books 2016

A catalogue record for this book is available from the National Library of Australia.

National Library of Australia Cataloguing-in-Publication entry:

Creator: Adolphs, Robin, author.
Title: Brave Danny / Robin Adolphs ; Nicky Johnston, illustrator.
ISBN: 9780994212139 (paperback)
Target Audience: For primary school age.
Subjects: Courage--Juvenile fiction.
Children's stories.
Other Creators/Contributors:
Johnston, Nicky, 1971-, illustrator.
Dewey Number: A823.4

This initiative is funded by the Australian Government.

Design and formatting services by BookCoverCafe.com

www.RobinAdolphs.com

First edition 2016
978-0-9942121-3-9 (pbk)
978-0-9942121-5-3 (e-bk)

Sometimes the smallest

voices are the most powerful.

Danny lay in bed pretending to be asleep.

He was sad. Dad was shouting at Mum again.

'Please stop,' Danny whispered.

But Dad kept shouting for a long time.

When he heard his mum start to cry
he knew his dad would stop and
everything would be quiet again.

The next morning Danny tiptoed into the kitchen. It was clean and tidy, but he could see pieces of broken plates in the corner.

Mum was sitting at the table silently without moving. Danny gave her a hug.

Danny's best friend Alex was waiting for him when he got to school.

'Hey, Danny, do you want to come for a sleepover tomorrow?' Alex asked.

Danny was excited. He'd never been on a sleepover before. He was a bit worried, too. He wondered what Alex's dad would be like.

Danny had fun all day on Saturday at Alex's house, jumping and running around.

He didn't feel afraid or sad. He felt like smiling and laughing.

Even dinnertime was fun.

That night Danny lay in bed waiting.

But all he heard were quiet voices talking and soft music playing.

'Your dad is cool,' Danny said. Maybe not all dads are like my dad, he

thought, as he drifted off to sleep.

Sunday afternoon came and it was time for Danny to go home.

That night, Danny lay in bed pretending to be asleep.

'I wish my dad was like Alex's dad,' he whispered to Rarfie.

At school the next day Mrs Foster asked, 'Do you all remember our special event today?'

'Yes, the life buoys are coming,' said Belle. 'They keep you safe in the water if you fall off a boat.'

'Ah, but these Life Buoys are different,' said Mrs Foster. 'They're actors and they're going to show you how to be safe everywhere.'

'Hello, everyone,' said the Life Buoys. 'Today we're going to have some fun with feelings.'

They sang a song and everyone clapped their hands.

'Now,' said Life Buoy One, 'how do you think I'm feeling?'

'You're happy,' said Tom. 'I know because you're smiling and cheering and jumping up and down.'

'You got it!' said Life Buoy One. 'High five.'

'What about me?' asked Life Buoy Two. He opened his eyes wide like big saucers and gasped.

'You're surprised,' said Sophie.

'You got it!' said Life Buoy Two. 'High five.'

One by one the children guessed how each Life Buoy was feeling.

Then it was Danny's turn.

'You're scared,' he said to Life Buoy Three. 'I know because you're crying and hiding your face. I bet you have butterflies in your tummy, too.'

'You got it!' Life Buoy Three said. 'High five.'

'Hands up anyone who's ever been afraid,' said Life Buoy Three.

Danny looked around as he raised his hand.

'Trust your feelings,' Life Buoy One said. 'It's okay to talk about your feelings because everyone needs to feel safe. Our good feelings tell us when we're safe, and our bad feelings tell us when something is …'

'WRONG!' everyone shouted.

When the Life Buoys had gone, Danny quietly told Mrs Foster that he was afraid of his dad.

Mrs Foster showed Danny a special handout the Life Buoys had given her.

'There's a lot of information in here about keeping safe,' she said.

Mum was waiting for Danny when he got home from school.

'Today we talked about our feelings and I drew a picture for you,' said Danny. 'Sorry it's a bit crumpled.'

'It's perfect,' said Mum.

'And the Life Buoys gave Mrs Foster special handouts for keeping safe,' said Danny.

'I'd like to see one of those too,' said Mum.

The next afternoon Danny heard his mum on the phone. She was talking about his dad and saying that she and Danny needed to feel safe again.

Somehow Danny knew that there were going to be big changes in his family soon. Maybe Dad wouldn't be living with them anymore.

He felt happy and sad at the same time.

That night when Danny's mum tucked him into bed, she said, 'You were very brave to talk about your feelings, Danny. You made me feel brave, too. Sometimes mums and dads just shouldn't be together.'

'Sleep tight, Rarfie, we're going to be safe now.'

For free-to-download Brave Danny notes, activities and worksheets, visit

www.robinadolphs.com

www.butternutbooks.com

Also visit

www.nickyjohnston.com.au

www.nrwc.com.au

A message from the National Rural Women's Coalition

Empowering the voices of our 'little people', like Danny, with his loyal companion, Rarfie, helps all of us to overcome one of the greatest human rights challenges of our time, family violence. Family violence is not an easy subject to speak about with young children. The effects on women and caregivers are well documented, but far less is known about the impact on the children—often the forgotten victims—who witness a parent being the subject of abuse. It can be frightening.

In 2016, the NRWC commissioned children's author, Robin Adolphs, to create a picture book for children aged 4 to 8 years. It tells the story of a young child in a domestic-violence situation being empowered, through a growing awareness of right and wrong, to make a difference. I am delighted that Robin and the illustrator, Nicky Johnston, have been able to bring this issue out from behind closed doors in such a sensitive and engaging way.

It is also worth noting that Robin has developed a guide to support the underlying messages inherent in the book to help parents and teachers when sharing the book with children.

It is the sincere hope of the NRWC that *Brave Danny* plays a strong role in helping some of our smallest victims.

Dr Pat Hamilton, president of the NRWC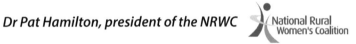

Acknowledgements

My sincerest thanks go to Dr Patricia Hamilton, president of the National Rural Women's Coalition, and the NRWC board, for commissioning me to write a children's picture book about domestic violence. It has been a privilege to write this story.

A very special thank you to Alwyn Friedersdorff, member of the NRWC board, for believing so strongly in this project, and for the commitment and support she afforded me throughout the process.

Children are often the silent victims of domestic violence, and I hope that Danny's story, although fictional, will help many children in abusive situations find their own strengths. So thank you, NRWC, for making me part of this wonderful project.

Sincere thanks also go to:

Dr Deborah Walsh, family violence specialist and lecturer at Queensland University, for sharing her time, expertise, knowledge and experience with me before I even began writing. Her help was invaluable.

Nicky Johnston, illustrator, not only for her beautiful illustrations, but also for being a great support throughout the writing of the book with her knowledge and compassion. And for breaking all deadlines!

Anthony Puttee and staff at Book Cover Cafe for the production of the book. Penny Springthorpe, editor, for invaluable advice and unending patience.

Jenny James for the notes and activities that accompany the book.

To all the people I spoke to, both women and men, who themselves have been victims of domestic violence, thank you for sharing your personal stories with me. And finally, thank you to everyone who listens to the smallest voices. They indeed have something to say.

Robin Adolphs

Also from Butternut Books

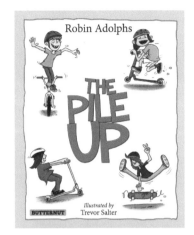

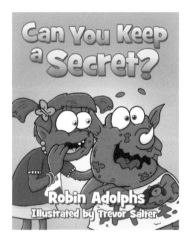

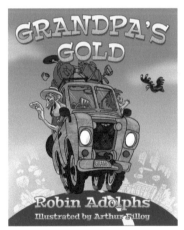

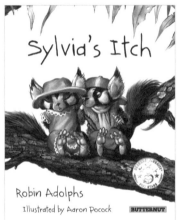

For more of Robin's books and free activities, visit

www.RobinAdolphs.com